DOMINIKA LIPNIEWSKA

DOODLE TOWN

TATE PUBLISHING

Welcome to Doodle Town, the place where everything and everyone is a drawing.

Get your pencils and pens ready: there are oodles of doodles waiting for you to bring them to life!

The residents of Doodle Town change their clothes simply by re-drawing them.

Design new outfits for these people and introduce them to your own characters. Will you be among them?

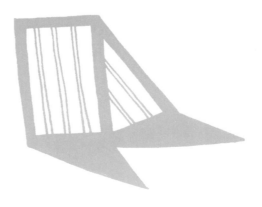

Design a statue for the town centre that will make people laugh.

The Doodle Town gardeners need your help!
Cover the town park with wild and wonderful plants. Use the flower-shaped stencil to get you started.

The Doodle Town cake shop usually looks delicious but today the baker has run out of icing.
Decorate the cakes with doodles and draw more treats to fill the shop.

Meet the Zig-Zag family: they love climbing up hills, mountains, stairs, and ladders.
Design them a house where they can climb all day.

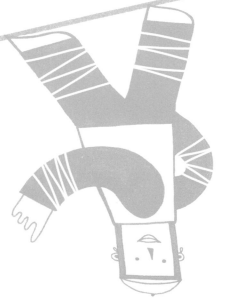

What do you love doing? Design your own house right next door.

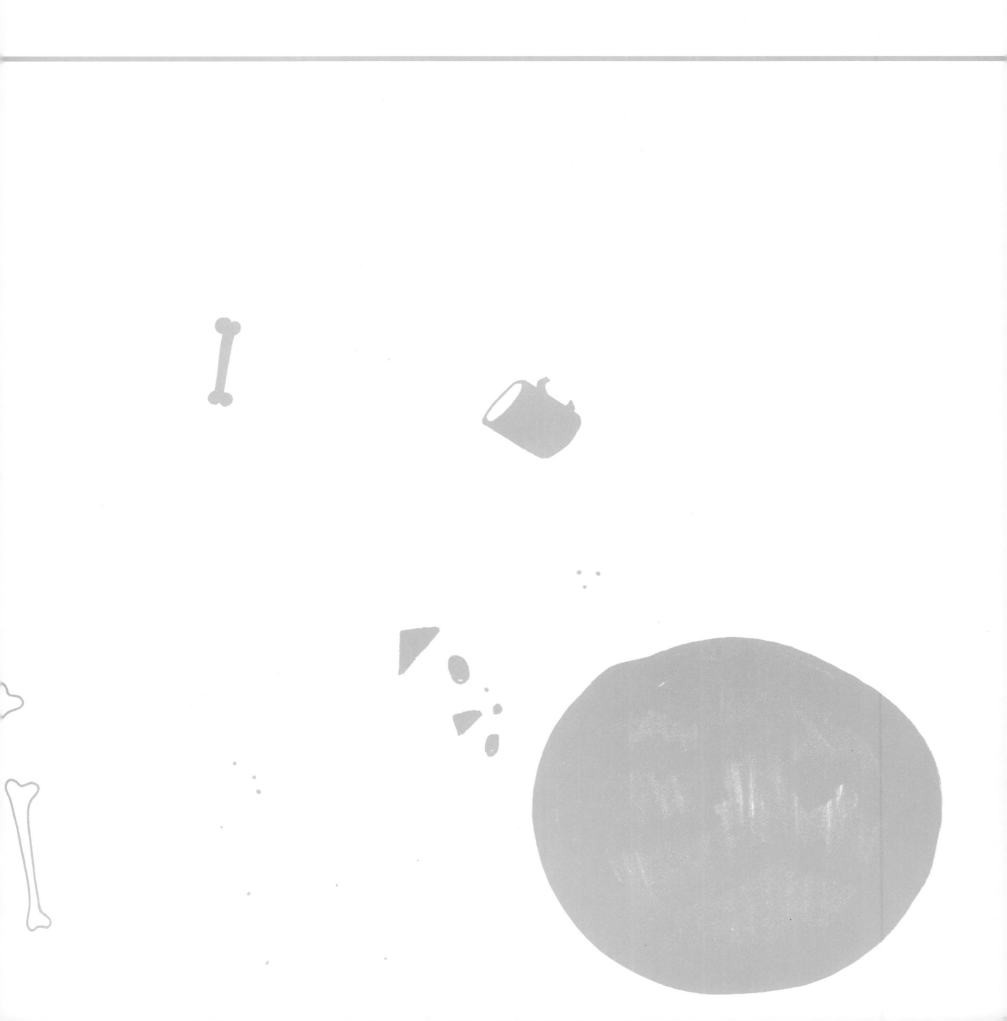

This is where the residents throw away their unwanted doodles.

Do you have any you'd like to add?

Wow, that's high! Here from the highest tower everything looks so small.
Use your sharpest pencil to draw a detailed view.

The show is about to start! Transform these shapes into performing puppets.

What a long train! What is it carrying, passengers or goods?

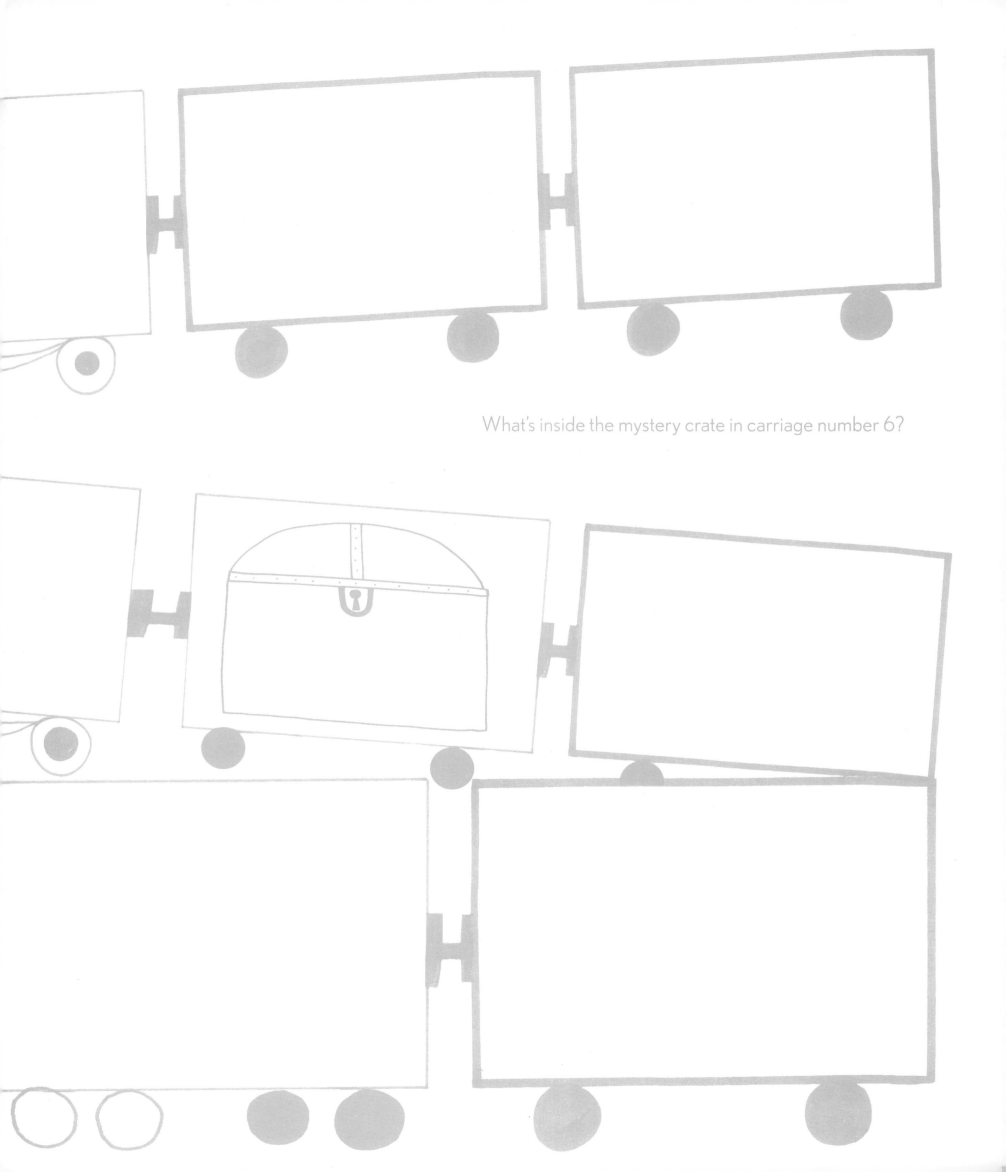

What's inside the mystery crate in carriage number 6?

The weather forecast predicts purple clouds with spotted rain.

Is it correct?

Fill the sky with doodles of weather. Use the cloud stencil to create lots of clouds quickly.

Doodle Town's most famous hair salon is so busy today they need an assistant!
Create some head-turning hairstyles for these customers.

The power lines above Doodle Town are where all the birds meet to chat.
Fill the lines with make-believe birds and imagine the noise they are making!

It's a beautiful sunny day down at the port.

Draw the shipyard's reflection in the river. You might want to turn the book upside down!

Welcome to the annual art exhibition!

The artists need your help creating some exciting pictures.

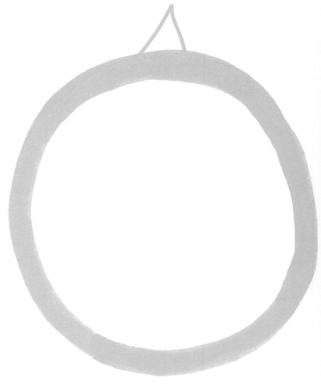

WoW!

I like this one!

Today is the Doodle Town Festival of Flying.
Finish the town skyline and fill the air with things that can fly.

It's a busy day at the market.

Can you find the items from the shopping list and draw them in the bag?

2 APPLES, 1 POT OF HERBS, 3 BANANAS, BEST CAKE, 1 SLICE of CHEESE, SMALL PICTURE FRAME, JAR OF... SOMETHING...

What do people eat in Doodle Town?

Scribble spaghetti or pencil shaving crisps, perhaps? Pile up this plate!

This playground is way too boring!
Invent fun new swings, slides and merry-go-rounds for everyone to play on.

The Doodle Town tailor has just heard that pattern is in fashion this season.
Help him re-design his latest collection before it goes on sale.

VOGE

Imagine the Doodle Town car park packed with fantastical vehicles.
What would a stair-climbing scooter or a seven-wheeled bicycle look like?